To all who dance to the beat of a different drummer. —N. W.

For my girls: Lola, Margo, and Anais. —H. D.

STERLING CHILDREN'S BOOKS
New York

An Imprint of Sterling Publishing Co., Inc.
1166 Avenue of the Americas
New York, NY 10036

ISBN 978-1-4549-2239-1

Library of Congress Cataloging-in-Publication Data

Names: Wing, Natasha, author. | Dardik, Helen, illustrator.
Title: Bagel in love / by Natasha Wing ; illustrated by Helen Dardik.
Description: New York : Sterling Children's Books, [2018] | Summary: Bagel
   wants to compete in a dance contest, but everyone from Pretzel to
   Croissant turns him down until, at last, shy and lovely Cupcake agrees to
   be his partner.
Identifiers: LCCN 2017021375 | ISBN 9781454922391 (book / hc-plc with jacket
   picture book)
Subjects: | CYAC: Bagels--Fiction. | Baked products--Fiction. |
   Dance--Fiction. | Contests--Fiction. | Humorous stories.
Classification: LCC PZ7.W72825 Bag 2018 | DDC [E]--dc23
LC record available at https://lccn.loc.gov/2017021375

Distributed in Canada by Sterling Publishing Co., Inc.
c/o Canadian Manda Group, 664 Annette Street
Toronto, Ontario M6S 2C8, Canada
Distributed in the United Kingdom by GMC Distribution Services
Castle Place, 166 High Street, Lewes, East Sussex BN7 1XU, England
Distributed in Australia by NewSouth Books
University of New South Wales, Sydney, NSW 2052, Australia

For information about custom editions, special sales, and premium and corporate purchases,
please contact Sterling Special Sales at 800-805-5489 or specialsales@sterlingpublishing.com

Manufactured in China

Lot #:
2 4 6 8 10 9 7 5 3
10/19

sterlingpublishing.com

Design by Jo Obarowski
The artwork for this book was created digitally.

BAGEL IN LOVE

by Natasha Wing   illustrations by Helen Dardik

STERLING CHILDREN'S BOOKS
New York

Bagel loved to dance. It made him happier than a birthday cake!
He never felt plain when he was spinning and swirling, tapping and twirling.

But he didn't have a partner, so he couldn't enter the dance contest.

DANCE CONTEST TONIGHT BRING YOUR PARTNER TO THE CHERRY JUBILEE PRIZES!!

Bagel asked the best dancer he knew in Bakersville to be his partner.

Poppy told him his dance steps were half-baked.

He asked Pretzel, who was at the spa getting a salt rub. She told him his moves didn't cut the mustard.

Matzo flat out told him no.

NO

Bagel didn't give up.
He knew there had to be *someone*
out there who'd love to dance with him.

With a hop, skip, and a pirouette,
Bagel set off to Sweet City.

He waltzed up to a table at a busy café.
"I bet you're all fabulous dancers."

Croissant rolled her eyes.
"Are you trying to butter us up?"

"Actually," said Bagel, "I'm looking for a partner
for the Cherry Jubilee dance contest."

Bagel tap-danced like the famous Fred Éclair.

CHECK out

THESE FANCY Feet!

"Call me flaky," said Croissant.
"But those moves are totally stale."

**He held out his hand to Doughnut.
"How about you?"**

Doughnut just stared at him, her eyes glazed over.

"Make like a mixer and beat it," said Cake.

Bagel felt dumped like yesterday's rolls.

He didn't give up. With all his courage, Bagel hopped onto a pedestal.

"Whoever can match me step for step, I'll take to the Cherry Jubilee!"

While Bagel tap-danced, Croissant, Doughnut, and Cake pointed and laughed. No one stepped forward to dance with him.

Soon the café emptied out—everyone had gone to watch the contest.
He climbed down from the pedestal. "Maybe next year," he whispered sadly.

Bagel stood outside
the empty café all alone.

He heard music coming from
the Cherry Jubilee.

His feet started tapping again.
To his surprise, he heard a reply.

He tapped again. Tap-tippity-tippity-tap-tap-tap.
Tap-tippity-tippity-tap-tap-tap came the response.

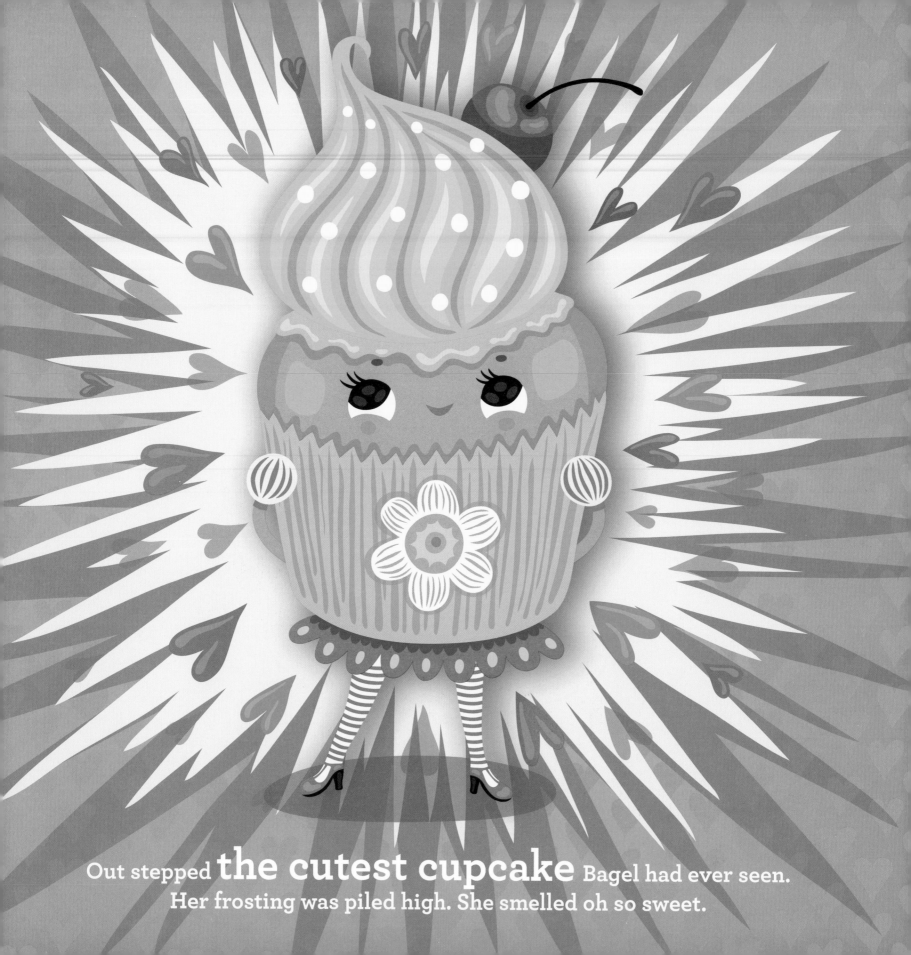

Out stepped **the cutest cupcake** Bagel had ever seen.
Her frosting was piled high. She smelled oh so sweet.

"Was that you I heard dancing?" asked Bagel.
"Yes," said Cupcake. "But I'm not very good."

"You sounded pretty good to me.
I bet you're better than you think!" said Bagel.
"Shall we give it a whirl?"

Bagel spun her around and around. Then he tossed her
in the air and caught her in his arms.
They ended in a dip, gazing into each other's eyes.

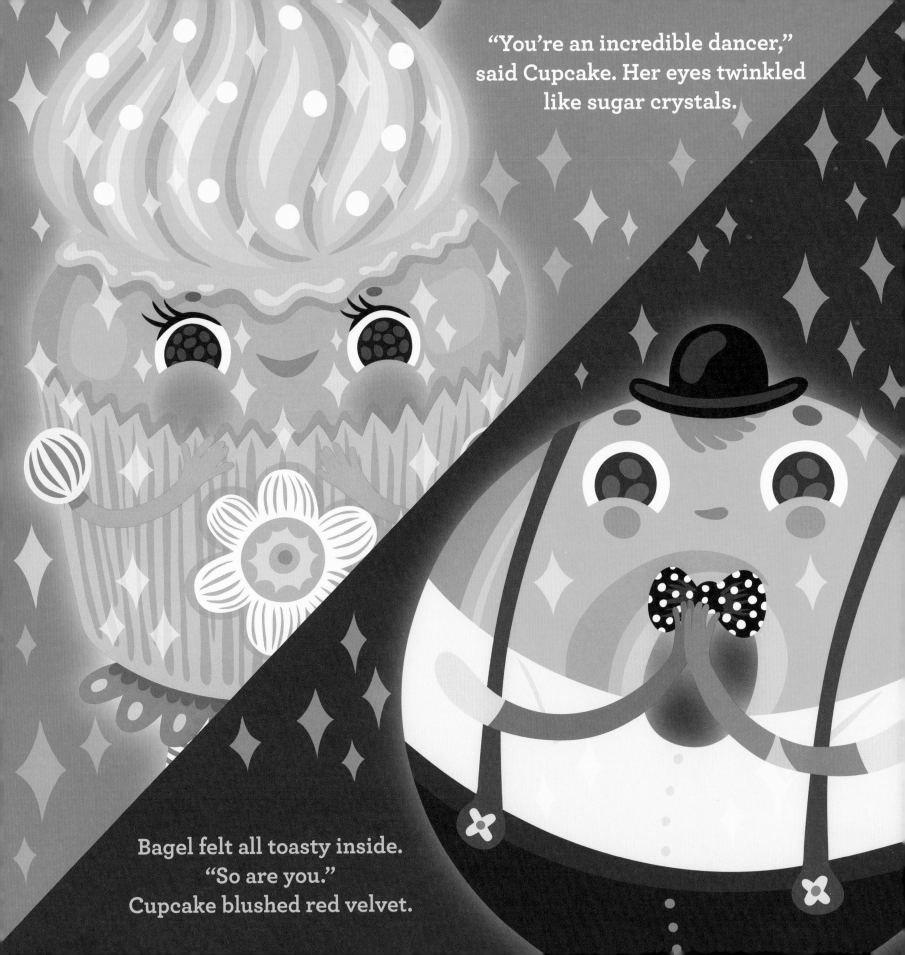

"You're an incredible dancer," said Cupcake. Her eyes twinkled like sugar crystals.

Bagel felt all toasty inside.
"So are you."
Cupcake blushed red velvet.

"Would you be my partner at the dance contest?" he asked.
"Pretty please with a cherry on top?"

They raced off to the Cherry Jubilee
just in time to enter the contest.

Bagel and Cupcake danced circles around the other contestants. Their fancy moves wowed the judges.

But for **Bagel** and **Cupcake**, winning the grand prize trophy was just **icing** on the **cake**.